EARLY BIRD
STORIES

The Great Grizzly Race

Early ★ Reader

First American edition published in 2019 by Lerner Publishing Group, Inc.

An original concept by Zoa Lumsden
Copyright © 2020 Zoa Lumsden

Illustrated by Monika Suska

First published by Maverick Arts Publishing Limited

Maverick
arts publishing

Licensed Edition
The Great Grizzly Race

Lerner Publications Company
A division of Lerner Publishing Group, Inc.
241 First Avenue North
Minneapolis, MN 55401 USA

For reading levels and more information, look up this title at
www.lernerbooks.com.

Main body text set in Mikado. Typeface provided by HVD Fonts.

Library of Congress Cataloging-in-Publication Data

Names: Zoa (Zoa Lumsden), author. | Suska, Monika, illustrator.
Title: The great grizzly race / by Zoa Lumsden ; illustrated by Monika Suska.
Description: Minneapolis : Lerner Publications, [2019] | Series: Early bird readers.
    Purple (Early bird stories) | "The original picture book text for this story has
    been modified by the author to be an early reader." | Originally published in
    Horsham, West Sussex by Maverick Arts Publishing Ltd. in 2017.
Identifiers: LCCN 2018043863 (print) | LCCN 2018052763 (ebook) |
    ISBN 9781541561755 (eb pdf) | ISBN 9781541542310 (lb)
Subjects: LCSH: Readers (Primary) | Grizzly bear—Juvenile literature. | Bicycle
    racing—Juvenile literature. | Bullying—Juvenile literature.
Classification: LCC PE1119 (ebook) | LCC PE1119 .Z73 2019 (print) |
    DDC 428.6/2—dc23

LC record available at https://lccn.loc.gov/2018043863

Manufactured in the United States of America
1-45405-39039-9/26/2018

EARLY BIRD
STORIES

The Great Grizzly Race

Zoa Lumsden

**Illustrated by
Monika Suska**

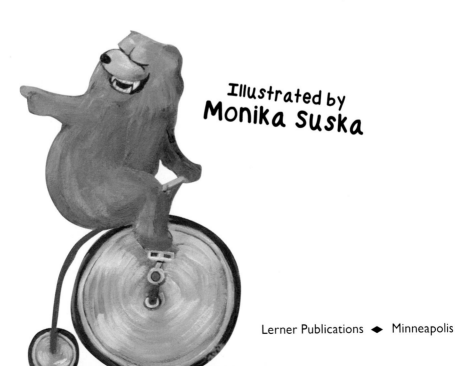

Lerner Publications ◆ Minneapolis

If you travel far, far north, you will find the wild land of Canada.

Watch out! Beware! Please take good care.

If you come here you might see a grizzly bear!

One lazy afternoon, the biggest, meanest grizzly of all caught a weasel eating his berries. "Give me one good reason why I should not eat you!" roared the grizzly.

"I have news of strangers!" squeaked the weasel.

"I saw two dogs on bikes."

"Strangers in MY valley?" said the grizzly.

"Not for long!"

Nearby, the Dog Detectives,

Detective Jack and Deputy Poco,

were roasting marshmallows, when . . .

. . . out of the woodpile jumped Penny Beaver!

"Oww! Oww!" she yelled. "My tail is on FIRE!"

She put her tail in the river to put out the flames.

"Your campfire used to be my house!" said Penny.

"Now where will I hide?"

"What are you hiding from?" asked Deputy Poco.

"The biggest, meanest grizzly of all," said Penny.

"That bully has stolen everyone's bikes so he can win the great race."

"Jump on, Penny!" said Detective Jack.

"We'll get your bikes back in time for the race."

The Dog Detectives rode off, deep into the valley.

They honked their horns and shouted, "Come out, everyone. Let's find the missing bikes!"

The animals searched until they found

a poop clue. Penny sniffed and sneezed,

"Achoooooo! Pepper always makes me sneeze."

"We must be getting close," said Deputy Poco.

"Only grizzly poop has a peppery smell!"

The trail led to muddy bicycle tracks.

But where were the missing bikes?

High above their heads, a duck said,

"Quack. Quack. QUACK!"

Everyone looked up and saw the bikes hanging in the trees.

"Hot diggity hotdogs!" said Detective Jack.

"Let's get the bikes down before the griz . . ."

The grizzly let out a big ROAR! All of the animals ran away except the Dog Detectives.

"I've met braver mice than you, grizzly," said Detective Jack. "You stole everyone's bikes because you are afraid to lose."

"I'm not afraid of anything," boasted the grizzly.

"I'll see you wimps at the great race tomorrow!"

So the next morning, the riders were off

and the great race began.

Up, up, and up they went. Who would win?

The grizzly was fast and he took the lead.

But soon the grizzly got tired and decided
to cheat. So at the top of the mountain,
he pushed over a tree.

What a disgrace! The grizzly had ruined the race!

He whizzed down the mountain, ready to win.

But everything changed when he hit a huge . . .

...rock!

CRASH! SMASH!

The grizzly cried out for help.

But . . . nobody wanted to help a bully.

"Come on," said Detective Jack.

"Let's show this grizzly how good it

feels to have friends."

Together they pulled the grizzly up.

For once, he did not try to bully them.

Instead, he smiled and cheered the

REAL winners of the Great Grizzly Race!

Quiz

1. What creatures must you beware of in the wildest wilderness?
   a) Horses
   b) Bears
   c) Beaver

2. Where were the missing bikes?
   a) Deep in a hole
   b) Hidden in a shed
   c) High in the trees

3. What does the grizzly use to block the path during the race?
   a) A tree
   b) A rock
   c) A bicycle

4. What animal has its tail on fire
   in the story?
   a) A weasel
   b) A beaver
   c) A duck

5. Why does nobody want to help
   the grizzly?
   a) He is a bully.
   b) He is smelly.
   c) The don't want him to win
      the race.

COLOR		GRL
Purple		J-K
Orange		H-J
Green		G-I
Blue		E-G
Yellow		C-E
Red		C-D
Pink		A-C

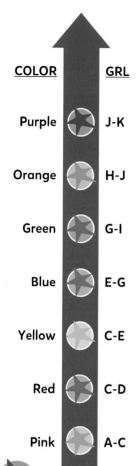

Leveled for Guided Reading

Early Bird Stories have been edited and leveled by leading educational consultants to correspond with guided reading levels. The levels are assigned by taking into account the content, language style, layout, and phonics used in each book.